The Mirror of Deception

Collect all the Charmseekers -

The Queen's Bracelet
The Silver Pool
The Dragon's Revenge
A Tale of Two Sisters
The Fragile Force
The Stolen Goblet
The Magic Crystals
Secret Treasure
Star Island
Moonlight and Mermaids
The Mirror of Deception
Zorgan and the Gorsemen

from March 2012
The Last Portal

www.charmseekers.co.uk

CHARMSEEKERS: BOOK ELEVEN

The Mirror of Deception

Georgie Adams

Illustrated by Gwen Millward

Orion
Children's Books

First published in Great Britain in 2009
by Orion Children's Books
Reissued 2012 by Orion Children's Books
a division of the Orion Publishing Group Ltd
Orion House
5 Upper St Martin's Lane
London WC2H 9EA
An Hachette UK Company

1 3 5 7 9 8 6 4 2

A catalogue record for this book is
available from the British Library.

ISBN 978 1 4440 0299 7

Printed and bound by
CPI Group (UK) Ltd, Croydon CR0 4YY

www.orionbooks.co.uk
www.charmseekers.co.uk

For Charlotte and Chris — with love

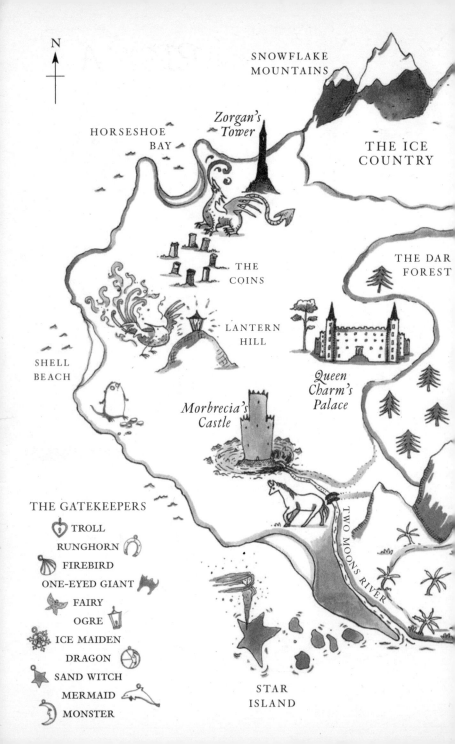

KARISMA

CAPE
CAT

CLOVER FIELDS

HEARTMOOR

DOLPHIN BAY

MOUNT
ORTUNA

The Silver Pool

KEY
POINT

SWAMPS

JUNGLE

MERMAID
ROCK

BUTTERFLY BAY

The Thirteen Charms of Karisma

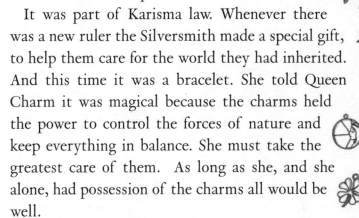

When Charm became queen of Karisma, the wise and beautiful Silversmith made her a precious gift. It was a bracelet. On it were fastened thirteen silver amulets, which the Silversmith called 'charms', in honour of the new queen.

It was part of Karisma law. Whenever there was a new ruler the Silversmith made a special gift, to help them care for the world they had inherited. And this time it was a bracelet. She told Queen Charm it was magical because the charms held the power to control the forces of nature and keep everything in balance. She must take the greatest care of them. As long as she, and she alone, had possession of the charms all would be well.

And so it was, until the bracelet was stolen by a spider, and fell into the hands of Zorgan, the magician. Then there was chaos!

One

One morning, not long after Sesame's last visit to Karisma, Queen Charm invited her good friend, the Silversmith, to the palace.

"I've received a puzzling letter from one of my gatekeepers," said Charm, handing the Silversmith a parchment scroll.

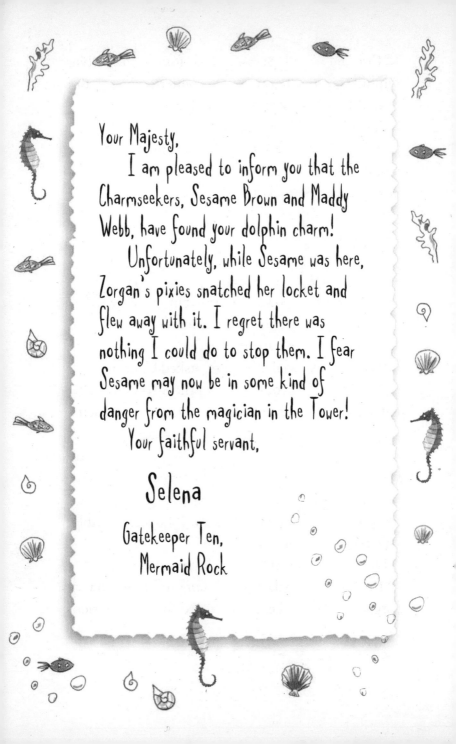

Your Majesty,

I am pleased to inform you that the Charmseekers, Sesame Brown and Maddy Webb, have found your dolphin charm!

Unfortunately, while Sesame was here, Zorgan's pixies snatched her locket and flew away with it. I regret there was nothing I could do to stop them. I fear Sesame may now be in some kind of danger from the magician in the Tower!

Your faithful servant,

Selena

Gatekeeper Ten,
Mermaid Rock

"I'm delighted Sesame has found my silver dolphin," said Charm. "It's wonderful news! But what's this about Zorgan and a locket?"

The Silversmith sighed.

"Your Majesty, I confess I've known about Zorgan's attempts to steal Sesame's locket for some time. But I didn't want to worry you. You've *quite* enough to think about! Once or twice I've used my mystic powers to prevent his pixies stealing it. Unfortunately this time I couldn't stop them."

"What's so special about it?" asked Charm.

"It's Sesame's favourite," said the Silversmith. "It matters to her a great deal. In possession of such a precious belonging Zorgan could . . ." She paused, knowing that what she was about to say would come as a shock. "Zorgan could enchant Sesame to make her bring him your bracelet!"

"Quisto!" * exclaimed Charm. "This is terrible! Isn't there *something* we can do?"

The Silversmith tried to calm her friend.

"I believe the locket is not *quite* so useful now to Zorgan as it might be. He appeared to me in a vision.

* *
Quisto – an exclamation of surprise

I saw him holding Sesame's locket. It was open. One of the pictures she keeps in it was missing. He looked furious."

Charm gave her a quizzical look; wondering whether she would *ever* understand her mysterious friend.

"What do you mean?" she asked.

"There's a chance the enchantment will fail," said the Silversmith. "But Zorgan won't give up easily. He'll have other tricks up his sleeve!"

A look of grim determination clouded Charm's delicate features.

"I've been patient too long," she said. "The future of Karisma is threatened by this slitey ✷ magician.

✷ ✷ ✷ ✷ ✷ ✷ ✷ ✷

✷ **Slitey** – sly or untrustworthy

He must be defeated! I'll call a Kluster* today. Please come. I should value your good advice."

Later that day, a group of important palace officials gathered round an enormous table in the State Room, discussing what to do about Zorgan. Seated on one side of Charm was the Silversmith, and on the other was her most trusted guard, Officer Dork.

There, too, was the Chancellor, a stout man called Robustus. He puffed out his cheeks and banged his fist on the table.

"Zorgan is a menace!" he stormed.

* *
Kluster – a meeting of important officials

7

"I agree," said the Prime Minister, a quietly spoken man with bright red hair and a beard. "The vermy * magician is indeed a menace. The cause of all our troubles."

"We need a plan," murmured the Head of the Planning Department. He had spent most of the meeting doodling on a pad with his quill pen. He had underlined the word 'PLAN' several times.

Officer Dork cleared his throat.

"Er, we could call out the army, Your Majesty," he suggested. "Finish Zorgan off, once and for all!"

The beautiful young queen looked from one to another, twisting a strand of fair hair round her finger.

"Surely we can stop him without resorting to violence," she said. "Things are bad enough without making them worse! The next time Sesame comes to Karisma, we must protect her. The sooner she finds all the charms and returns them to me, the better. Zorgan is powerful, but he's no match against my magical charm bracelet."

* *
* **Vermy** – miserable worm

8

"Yes," said the Silversmith. "Let's try to resolve this peacefully. But if all else fails, we may *have* to take Zorgan by force!

Two

Princess Morbrecia entered Zorgan's Tower and threw back the hood of her black, velvet cloak. The princess had covered herself from head to toe, so no one could recognise her. It would never do for the sister of Queen Charm to be seen visiting the wicked magician!

As Morbrecia climbed the one hundred and ninety-five twisty steps to the Star Room, she recalled her last visit to the tower, many medes* ago. She remembered that night as if it were yesterday . . .

* * * * * * * *
*Mede – month

I brought the bracelet to Zorgan, just as we'd planned. I risked everything, but I did it. He promised to empower it with Dark Magic and make me queen. But he ruined everything when he threw the charms away.

"I'll never forgive him, the magwort!" ✶ Morbrecia spat the last word. At the top of the stairs she paused to catch her breath, before opening the heavy wooden door to the Star Room. Stepping inside, her mood of displeasure quickly changed to delight.

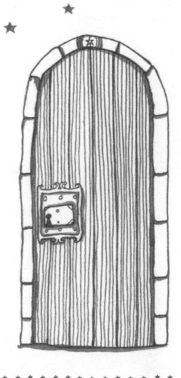

✶ **Magwort** – probably the worst name you could call anyone! General term for a fool

Since childhood Morbrecia had been fascinated by sorcery. It thrilled her to see the weird and wonderful things Zorgan used to make magic. Suspended from the ceiling was an amazing clockwork universe, with moons and planets whirling around the sun. Bottles of slime-green potions, fizzing, frothing and fit to explode, jostled for space on a shelf next to jars of jellied frogs, snakes' eyes and worms. Leather-bound spell books, a flickering black candle, one skull and a wand lay piled haphazardly on a table. Near a window stood Zorgan's telescope and, on a plinth, was his glowing crystal ball. Vanda, the magician's pet bandrall,* was perched on a chair. She eyed Morbrecia suspiciously.

Zorgan greeted Morbrecia with the thinnest of smiles.

"Welcome, Your Highness," he said, bowing.

* * * * * * * * * * * * * * * * *
Bandrall – rare flying mammal, native to Karisma

12

Morbrecia wasn't fooled by Zorgan's gesture of respect. She'd learned to be wary of the sly magician. But she wanted the bracelet more than anything and she needed his help to get it. Besides, only Zorgan could empower the charms with Dark Magic, which was *so* much more dangerous and exciting than white magic. She'd have fun causing havoc and mayhem! Her eye caught something silver, glistening in Zorgan's hand and she wondered if he'd found a missing charm.

"What's that?" she asked.

Zorgan showed her the necklace nestled on his palm.

"Sesame's locket!" exclaimed Morbrecia, recognising it at once. She'd tried to steal it herself on more than one occasion. "We have it at last. Quick! Put a curse on that interfering Outworlder." ✶

Zorgan frowned. He opened the locket and showed Morbrecia the empty space where there had once been two little photographs. Nic Brown smiled out at them, but Poppy Brown's picture was missing.

"Where is it?" asked Morbrecia.

* *
✶ **Outworld** – the name Karismans call our world

14

"My foolish pixies lost it at Mermaid Rock,"* said Zorgan. He glared at Nix and Dina, who were quivering in a corner. "I have severely punished them for their mistake. They were lucky I didn't turn them into fish paste! But what's done is done. I believe the gatekeeper found the picture and returned it to Sesame—"

"So?" snapped Morbrecia. "You still have the locket. What are we waiting for? Cast the spell!"

Morbrecia could barely contain her excitement as Zorgan prepared to perform the curse. From the toppling pile of spell books he selected a dusty tome:

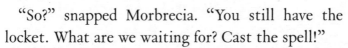

Curses Ancient and Modern.

* *

Mermaid Rock – do you remember what happened? You can read about Sesame's exciting adventure in Book Ten: *Moonlight and Mermaids*

He blew the dust from its cover, then tapped it with his wand and commanded:

"Open! Page two hundred and eighty-four."

As if by magic, the book opened at the right place. Zorgan held up Sesame's locket, gazed into his crystal ball and chanted:

"Oh, crystal ball reveal to me
The whereabouts of Sesame.
My spell shall make the Seeker see,
She must bring all the charms
to ME!"

Three

Sesame couldn't believe it. She had just come third in the Pole Bending event, riding Silver in her very first gymkhana.

"Well done, Ses!" said Nic Brown, as he walked over to the horsebox with his daughter. "I got a great photo of you racing over the finish line."

"Thanks, Dad," said Sesame, smiling happily. She gave Silver a pat; a bright yellow rosette was fluttering from his bridle.

Sesame's riding instructor, Jodie Luck, was there too. She beamed at Sesame.

"You were brilliant," she said. "You've worked so hard. Keep it up. You're my star pupil!"

When they reached the horsebox, Sesame got Silver ready for the journey back to Jodie's yard. She was putting on his travel rug, when she caught sight of Olivia Pike on her dappled-grey mare, Misty Morning. Olivia went to Sesame's school and kept her pony at Jodie's too. Sesame thought Olivia was a spoilt brat, because she never stopped bragging about owning her own pony. They were *not* the best of friends!

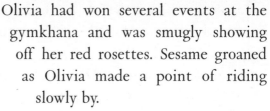

Olivia had won several events at the gymkhana and was smugly showing off her red rosettes. Sesame groaned as Olivia made a point of riding slowly by.

"Better luck next time, Sesame," she called out. "Bet you wish you could ride as well as me. *And* had a super pony like mine!"

"Silver is the best pony in the world," retorted Sesame hotly. "So there!"

Jodie heard and came over to calm things down. Olivia ambled off smirking, leaving Sesame fuming.

"I *know* I should have ignored her," she admitted to Jodie. "But Olivia is SO annoying!"

"Time to go, I think," said Jodie tactfully. "It's been a super day. Don't let *anyone* spoil it! Believe in yourself, Sesame. You did your best."

* * *

That evening, Jodie came to supper with Nic and Sesame, and stayed to watch a DVD. Jodie had been going out with Sesame's dad for several months; Sesame had grown very fond of her and the feeling was mutual – and they shared a love of horses!

18

Sesame glanced at the TV. Nic had put on an old-fashioned black and white film with romantic background music.

"Dad, what *are* you watching?" she said.

"*Moonlight Madness*," said Nic. "A classic."

"Mm," said Jodie, reaching for a box of tissues. "This one always makes me cry. I love it."

Sesame rolled her eyes.

"I'm going to chill," she said. "See you two later."

She went up to her room; Chips and Pins raced ahead to lie in wait for her under the bed. When they shot out to pounce on her feet, she skipped aside laughing, then proudly pinned up the photo of her and Silver that her dad had taken at the gymkhana. She put her yellow rosette beside it.

"Perhaps one day I'll ride in the Olympics," she told her teddy, Alfie, "and win a gold medal." She giggled. "If I won gold, Olivia Pike would go green with envy!"

Next she put on a CD – her favourite band, Crystal Chix – and went online to chat to her best friend, Maddy Webb. After they'd chatted about Sesame's gymkhana win for a while, Maddy said:

MadWebbgirl@mailwizard.net says:

I've got to wash my hair 2nite. Wot RU doing?

seekerSes@zoom.com says:

Chilling out. Dad and Jodie are watching a film. Moonlight Madness. Sooooo boring!

MadWebbgirl@mailwizard.net says:

Sounds romantic! Do you think your dad and Jodie will get married?

seekerSes@zoom.com says:

I don't know. Maybe.

MadWebbgirl@mailwizard.net says:

Cool! If they did, Jodie would be your new mum!

Sesame stared at her computer screen. The words 'new mum' jumped out at her. She'd never thought of anyone taking the place of her mother before.

MadWebbgirl@mailwizard.net says:

Ses, RU OK? Sorry if I said the wrong thing.☹

seekerSes@zoom.com says:

Yes, I'm fine. Honestly.☺ Jodie's great. I just never thought of her in that way.

MadWebbgirl@mailwizard.net says:

Oh, must go. Mum says I've got to wash my hair NOW. See U at SKL 2moz. Talk 2U then. Nite nite. Sleep tite. x

seekerSes@zoom.com says:

See you. Mwah Mwah xx

Sesame shut down her computer. Maddy's comment about Jodie set her thinking. How *would* I feel about having Jodie as my mum? I'm not sure. I was a baby when Poppy died. I don't remember much about her, but I think I'd feel guilty calling Jodie 'Mum'. Anyway, Dad and Jodie aren't even engaged! It may never happen.

Going to her bedside table, she opened her special jewellery box where she kept the magical charm bracelet and charms. They sparkled in the lamplight as she opened the box. She'd also placed the little photo of her mother from her locket there for safe-keeping and, seeing Poppy Brown's happy face, she picked up the photo and looked at it closely. Then, on impulse, she tucked it into her pocket. I might not have my locket, but I can still keep this close to me, she thought.

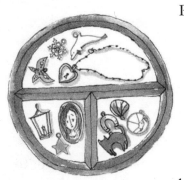

Sesame sighed. "I love Dad," she told Alfie, "and I can tell Gran *most* things. But perhaps it would be nice to have a mum . . ."

Seeing the bracelet and charms, Sesame thoughts quickly turned to Karisma. She'd found ten charms and was anxious to find the three that were still lost. Picking up the bracelet, she admired the one charm clinging to it – the perfect little heart with a lock.

"The queen lost her bracelet *ages* ago," she told Alfie. "She must be sad. I hope I can return it soon."

22

Almost without thinking, Sesame began to fasten the other charms to the bracelet; one by one she added the horseshoe, shell, cat, butterfly, snowflake, lantern, coin, star and dolphin. They twinkled like stars on a frosty night.

"Oh!" she exclaimed, her eyes shining with pleasure. "It's beautiful. I wish I had one like it."

Holding the bracelet, she became aware of a tingling sensation prickling the tips of her fingers. It reminded her of the way her locket used to tingle, when something extraordinary was about to happen. That was before Zorgan's nasty pixies had snatched it, the last time she was in Karisma. Nic and Lossy thought she'd lost it swimming at Water Wonderland. She couldn't tell them what had really happened. Was the charm bracelet trying to tell her something? she wondered.

Chips and Pins were acting strangely too. They were hissing at something in Sesame's wardrobe mirror; their fur stood on end and their tails bristled like brushes.

Without warning, a dazzling light streaked across the glass, as if it had been struck by lightning. Instinctively, Sesame shielded her eyes and the cats flew under the bed.

When she dared to look again, she gasped. Reflected in the mirror was a man dressed in a long, dark robe; and from his finger he dangled her locket. Sesame knew, without the shadow of a doubt, that she was looking at Zorgan!

Four

Sesame tried to scream, but she couldn't. She shut her eyes tight, then opened them again, hoping the vision had gone. But it was still there — real as anything.

Zorgan fixed her with his cold, black eyes. Slowly, rhythmically, the magician swung the locket like a pendulum — this way, that way, to and fro — so that almost immediately Sesame became mesmerised by the swaying movement. She felt herself drawn like a magnet to the magician, and all the time she could hear his haunting, hypnotic voice coaxing her to give him the charms:

"Bring me the charms.
Give them to me,
S-E-S-A-M-E-E-E!"

26

Dimly, she saw his hand reaching out to her. She felt weak and sleepy. Oh, so sleepy! Until . . .

Suddenly stars swirled from the bracelet! Dazed and confused, Sesame snapped out of the trance. Just in time she stepped back from the mirror.

"No! No!" she yelled. "The bracelet belongs to Queen Charm. I'll never give it you. Never!"

Thoughts raced inside her head. She *must* protect the bracelet at all costs! Slowly she backed across the room, not daring to take her eyes off Zorgan for a second. She dropped the bracelet in her jewellery box, then closed the lid with a *snap!* Phew! she thought. The charms are safe, I hope!

Zorgan was furious, but managed to hide his rage. It would never do for Sesame to think she'd won.

"Blatz!" ✻ he cursed, through gritted teeth. "The power of the bracelet has broken my hypnotic spell. But I'm not finished yet. I'll twist the truth to make Sesame see things *my* way. She'll bring me the charms of her own free will."

* *
✻ **Blatz** – a really angry exclamation

Zorgan smiled at the young girl who had confronted him so boldly, with arms folded and an expression of defiance on her face. He spoke quietly, his voice oozing false concern:

"Brave Sesame, you've been sadly misguided by the Silversmith. She is using you to carry out her plan. It is *her* you should fear, not me. When you've returned all the charms to the queen she will have no further use for you. She has tricked you and I fear your life is in danger."

Sesame listened, her heart thumping. She wished Maddy were here! She could hear Chips and Pins softly growling under the bed. She stood her ground. I'm not silly, she thought. Zorgan's faking.

"I don't believe you!" she shouted. "Go away!"

The image of Zorgan remained.

"Listen," he said, struggling to keep his temper under control. "The Silversmith is really a wicked witch! She's in disguise. She's cursed the charms. This notion about them controlling nature is nonsense. They're the *cause* of all the bad things happening in Karisma, and it's her doing!"

Sesame was horrified. This was the opposite of everything she'd been told. She was sure the magician must be telling lies.

"No way!" she said. "That's so not true."

"I'm afraid it is," said Zorgan. "The Silversmith is cunning. She befriended Queen Charm and made her the bracelet. She persuaded her it was a magical force for good. For a while all was well. But it was all part of the Silversmith's plan to cause misery and chaos."

Sesame looked puzzled.

"Why would she do that?" she challenged.

"The Silversmith wanted to create havoc," said Zorgan. "The witch has power over all things silver. She *controls* the charms! When it suited her, she intended to put her plan into action. Win the people's respect. Charm would appear weak and the witch would seize the throne."

Sesame thought Zorgan was beginning to sound convincing. Supposing he *was* telling the truth?

"What about Morbrecia?" asked Sesame. "I know she's after the charms."

"Morbrecia is the *true* queen of Karisma. She is the eldest princess," replied Zorgan. "She stole the bracelet from Charm to thwart the Silversmith. Morbrecia knew there was a chance I could break the curse, so she brought them to me.

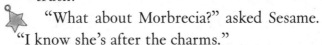

I tried and failed. So I cast them away. The Silversmith has used YOU to get them back—"

"How?" broke in Sesame. "I've never met her."

"The witch possesses mystic powers," said Zorgan. "She controls you through this…"

Zorgan held up her locket.

"Give it back!" cried Sesame. "It was your horrid pixies who stole it."

"For your own good," said Zorgan soothingly. "I *had* to stop the Silversmith communicating with you, before it was too late. Morbrecia tried to warn you too. Don't you see? If you return the bracelet to her sister, the Silversmith will have won. Your reward will be the witch's CURSE!"

Zorgan's last words boomed in Sesame's ears like thunder. She staggered, reeling from the shock of realising that, after all this time, she might have been under the spell of a wicked witch! It was chilling.

When she looked at the mirror again, the vision of Zorgan had vanished. In its place was a swirling mass of stars, drawing her into a whirlpool of golden light. Before she knew what was happening, the looking-glass melted away and she was spinning round and round, faster and faster, through a magical golden light . . .

Once more, Sesame was on her way to Karisma.

Five

Sesame tumbled through time, spinning in the vastness of space, until she drifted down across a silvery sea, to land –

BUMP

– on a beach. She picked herself up and looked around.

"I know I'm in Karisma," she said. "But I wonder where I am?"

She half expected to be met by a gatekeeper – that's what usually happened when she arrived in Karisma – but this time she was disappointed. There was no one about. Scrambling up the shingle to the foot of a cliff, she came to a rocky cavern; the entrance was barred by an iron gate, its rusty ironwork forged into a design of ferocious beasts, which Sesame thought looked very frightening. On one side, roughly chiselled into the rock was the number eleven, and on the other, the words:

RING IF YOU DARE!

Suddenly she remembered what she'd once been told about Gatekeeper Eleven – he was a monster who ate his visitors! She gulped at the thought, then realised she had to face him. "I must go through the gate, or I might not get out again. I hope the monster isn't hungry!"

She took a deep breath and rang the bell . . .

clang! Clang!
Clang!

"WHO'S THERE?"

boomed a voice, so loud and fierce it made Sesame jump. She felt like making a run for it, but didn't. Instead she called out:

"Sesame Brown!" and her name reverberated round the walls.

Sesame Brown . . .
Sesame Brown . . .
Sesame Brown . . .

"WHAT DO YOU WANT?"

came the reply.

"I've c-c-come to look for the ch-charms," stammered Sesame, her knees knocking. "I'm a Charmseeker!"

There was a pause, then:

"COME IN!"

The gate swung open by itself, and Sesame stepped inside a huge cave, dimly lit by lanterns.

"Anyone there?" she called out nervously.

At the sound of shuffling feet, she turned and was astonished to see a weird-looking creature, only half her size. He had an extraordinarily large head, bulging eyes and a body covered in purplish skin, attached to which was a tail. In one hand he held a speaking-trumpet.

"Quinch," he said, extending a skinny arm

to shake Sesame by the hand. "Welcome to Karisma!"

Sesame was flabbergasted. She couldn't believe this pathetic creature had nearly frightened her to death! Quinch must have read her thoughts.

"I'm not fierce," he confessed. "I use this to scare people." He put the trumpet to his lips.

WOOOOOAAAH!

"Scary, huh?"

Sesame rolled her eyes.

"Yeah, great," she said. "Er, by the way, I've heard you . . . eat people. You call them your *elevenses*."

Quinch squinted at her through bulbous eyes.

"Who told you that?" he said.

"The troll at Gate One," said Sesame.

Quinch laughed and slapped his sides.

"I know that troll," he said. "He likes a good joke. No, of course not. Me, eat people? Yuk! But don't tell anyone. You'll ruin my reputation!"

Just then his tummy rumbled loudly.

"All this talk of food has made me hungry," he said. "Time for buttered beans. Would you like some?"

"No, thank you," said Sesame politely. She thought she'd wasted enough time already. "I must look for the charms. The moon, the clover leaf and the key are still missing. Sesame Brown will track them down!"

Quinch led the way up a flight of stone steps, which zigzagged crazily inside the cliff. When they reached the top, they stepped out into warm, mid-morning sunshine.

"Phew!" said Sesame, slightly out of breath. "Where are we?"

"Shell Beach," said Quinch, indicating the beach where Sesame had landed far below. She could see some familiar places too: Lantern Hill, Charm's Palace, Morbrecia's Castle . . . and, away in the distance, a soaring column of black rock. Zorgan's Tower! Although it was daytime, Sesame was fascinated to see two crescent moons shining brightly above the tower. The way the moons were positioned in the sky reminded her of the Charmseekers' secret hand sign! She was sure it was a clue, and quickly showed Quinch what she meant.

"Perhaps I'll find the *moon* charm at Zorgan's Tower!" she told the gatekeeper.

Quinch looked horrified.

"No one goes there," he said.

"Well, I have to," said Sesame firmly. "What time does the gate close?"

"Listen for the bell," said Quinch. "You must return before it strikes eleven. Setfair!* And watch out for the magician!"

* *
✴ Setfair – goodbye and good luck

Six

Meanwhile, in his Star Room, Zorgan had spotted Sesame through his powerful telescope. He'd failed to hypnotise her, but he was determined to think of some other way to persuade her to bring him the charms. And Morbrecia was impatient for results.

"Your stupid spell didn't work!" complained the princess, who'd been with him all the while. "What now?"

"Smoke and mirrors," murmured the magician, ideas whirling inside his head. "Shades and shadows cloud her eyes . . . a feathered friend . . . a maze of lies!"

"What *are* you talking about?" snapped Morbrecia.

"Listen," said Zorgan. "Here's what we'll do . . ."

On this particular
morning, in the
eleventh mede
of Kaleg, the
Silversmith is
thinking about
Sesame too. She
is walking on Mount
Fortuna and notices the
two moons above Zorgan's
Tower. She knows it is the time of
year when the moons shine especially bright,
but something about their appearance gives her
cause for concern. Weeks have passed since the
Kluster at the palace, at which Charm had given
orders for plans to be drawn up to
take Zorgan by force, if need be.
Officer Dork and his men were to
protect Sesame when she returned,
but as yet there has been no sign
of her. The Silversmith has spent
many anxious days waiting for her
Seeker to return, but she knows it's
not something she can hurry. Seeing
the moons strangely positioned over
the tower, she wonders if this is a sign.
I fear Sesame may soon be in danger,
she thinks.

Quickly she runs down the mountainside and enters her workshop. Straightaway her gaze falls upon the thirteen magic candles; three burn steadfastly for their missing charms.

"I'll do what I can to protect Sesame," she whispers to the candles. "Only three more charms to find. She *must* finish her quest. I can't let Zorgan win!"

She lights a tinder-stick of mystica* and before long, the air is filled with its fragrant aroma. It calms her, as she prepares to use her mystic powers.

Seating herself at a small elegant table, she places her fingertips lightly on its surface and closes her eyes. Soon she's in a trance and fleeting images from the past, present and future flit through her head like moths in the moonlight . . .

"I see the bracelet," she murmurs. "The power of the charms defeated the magician. Good! Ah, my Seeker is here. I see her with a bird. I see . . . a *magic mirror*! What is Zorgan's plan? He will stop at nothing."

* *
Mystica – an aromatic plant, native to Karisma. The petals produce a sweet smell when burned

The vision fades and the Silversmith opens her eyes.

"There's no time to lose. I must call upon the Moon Spirits. I know they will help, if they can."

⁂

Sesame set off along the cliffs, heading north, following a path by the sea. It was summer and the sun felt hot on her back as she walked along, deep in thought. She was thinking about the vision of Zorgan in her wardrobe mirror; he'd said some disturbing things and they came back to haunt her now . . .

"Zorgan said the Silversmith is really a wicked witch. She cursed the charms and wants to rule Karisma. If I return the bracelet to Queen Charm, I'll be helping the Silversmith to cause chaos. Is Zorgan telling the truth? Perhaps not. I know *he* wants the bracelet. And why have I never met the Silversmith? Is she hiding something? What about Queen Charm? Oh, I don't know. Zorgan says Morbrecia is the *true* queen. Is she? That would explain why he wants the bracelet, to give to her. It's very confusing!"

Sesame plunged her hands into her pockets and felt the photo of Poppy there, which was reassuring. She remembered her mother had been a journalist, investigating stories. She wondered what Poppy would make of this!

Sesame went on mulling things over, trying to make sense of it all. Once or twice, she had the uncanny feeling that Zorgan was near; she kept looking over her shoulder to see if he was there, but it seemed she was alone. Before long she came to Horseshoe Bay, where the path divided and she turned right, towards the tower. With a twinge of unease, she saw it was not far away – and again and again she sensed a supernatural presence, although she could see nothing.

The sun was hotter than ever. Her throat felt tight and dry and suddenly Sesame felt *very* thirsty. By a curious coincidence, just as she was thinking how desperate she was for some water, she came to a spring, bubbling from a rock. She cupped her hands beneath the flow and drank – gulping mouthfuls of crystal clear water.

"Brill!" she exclaimed, wiping the drips from her chin with the back of her hand.

As she did so, she was startled by the *swish* of wings. For a split-second, a shadowy shape blotted out the sun and, glancing up, Sesame gave a little cry.

44

Perched on the rock and watching her every move was a huge, black crow.

Sesame recovered quickly. It was only a bird, and the spring water had refreshed her. She felt much better. She thought the crow looked magnificent, with his shiny blue-black beak and gleaming feathers. She was delighted when he spoke.

"Feeling better?" said the crow, cocking his head at the spring. "Cool water on a hot day. Nothing better! Where are you going?"

Sesame pointed to the tower.

"I'm looking for the lost charms," she told him. "I think I'll find the moon charm there."

"Ah," said the crow, sharp eyes glinting. "I hope you find it. You must allow me to show you the way."

"Thanks!" said Sesame. "Have you met the magician? There's loads I'd like to know about him."

"I know Zorgan well," said the crow, a crafty smile turning the corners of his beak. "We shall talk as we go along."

So the two set off.

Since drinking the water, Sesame had been feeling a *little* light-headed. "Probably too much sun," she said to herself, and she thought no more of it. Soon, she was happily chatting to her companion, telling the crow all about the Charmseekers and her quest to find the charms.

For his part, the crow spoke favourably about Zorgan and, with every step of the way, Sesame grew more and more convinced the magician might be someone she could trust. But as they approached the tower, Sesame noticed a chill in the air and shivered. The sun wasn't shining any more and nothing grew in these parts – not even a blade of grass. Sesame thought Zorgan's Tower looked spooky in the moonlight as they walked in its long, dark shadow and soon they were standing at the magician's door.

Seven

The tower rose from the bleak landscape like a serpent ready to strike. Above it hung the crescent moons, like a Charmseekers' sign in the sky.

Goosebumps prickled Sesame's skin. Despite the crow's reassurances about Zorgan, she couldn't help feeling a bit afraid now that she was there. Close up, the tower *did* look scary! Turning to the crow, she was dismayed to find she was alone. The crow had disappeared. He had simply vanished into thin air.

"Okay," Sesame told herself. "Don't be silly. Hurry up and look for the charm!"

She decided to start at the door and search around the base of the tower.

But when she looked, the door wasn't there! In its place was a shimmering mirror, giving off an eerie, green glow. She went and stood right in front of the mirror, expecting to see her own image reflected in the glass, but instead she saw twinkling fairy lights and could hear the sound of music and laughter. As she reached to touch the mirror, to see if it was real, the glass melted – and she stepped through a magical mist. In the distance she heard the bell strike six.

Clang! Clang! Clang! Clang!

Clang! Clang! Clang!

To Sesame's surprise, waiting for her on the other side of the mirror, was Morbrecia. She smiled and took Sesame gently by the hand.

"Don't be afraid," said Morbrecia. "I'm going to show you what happened a long time ago. Maybe then you'll see how the Silversmith has tricked you. Believe me, you're in great danger!"

Sesame couldn't believe her ears. Surely this wasn't the scheming princess she'd come up against before? *This* Morbrecia was friendly!

"R-i-g-h-t," said Sesame. "Where are we going?"

"To a party," said Morbrecia. "Follow me!"

It all begun at Charm's seventh birthday party. I was nine. I'm two years older than my sister. We were so excited because Zorgan the Court Magician was giving a Magic Show. But that day something happened to spoil everything!

A fairy called Quilla came to see my parents, King Orin and Queen Amilla.

50

The Silversmith sent her, to tell them a silly story about me. Quilla said my name began with the letter 'M' and it was a BAD omen! 'M' upside-down turns into 'W' and stands for Wicked Witch! So she told my parents I should never become queen. Charm must wear the crown, not ME! And they believed Quilla. When Zorgan told me, I was very upset. It wasn't fair. I'm the eldest. I should be queen of Karisma!

Hm! I can see why Morbrecia is so angry.

The party scene faded into a foggy haze. When it cleared, Sesame was standing by a deep pool full of silver. She stared at the vision in awe.

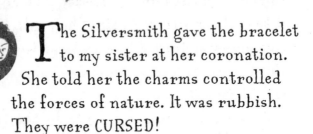

The Silversmith gave the bracelet to my sister at her coronation. She told her the charms controlled the forces of nature. It was rubbish. They were CURSED!

On the eve of Charm's coronation, the Silversmith took the charm bracelet and dipped it three times in the Silver Pool. Then she invoked the spirit of Agapogo the dragon, to breath fire on it to seal the curse. Against her will, Agapogo was forced to obey the witch. But the dragon vowed one day she would seek revenge.

I'm afraid Charm was fooled by the Silversmith. She was taken in by her mystic mumblings! But I tell you, Sesame, the Silversmith means you harm. Once you've returned the charms, you'll be of no further use to her. She will be rid of you!

Oh dear! It looks like the Silversmith *is* a witch!

The image wavered, then faded in a misty cloud. Sesame blinked and the scene changed again. This time she was in Zorgan's Star Room, on the night he threw the charms away.

I managed, only by putting myself in great danger, to take the bracelet from Charm because the Silversmith had unleashed the curse. The charms were causing misery and chaos!

It was all part of her plan. When it suited her, she was going to take control of the charms and restore order. My sister would appear weak, whereas the witch would gain everyone's respect. Before long she would have overthrown Charm and seized the throne!

Anyway, I took the bracelet to Zorgan to break the curse. He tried all kinds of spells but nothing worked. So he threw the charms from the tower to disperse their Dark Energy.

The charm bracelet IS beautiful.
I would love to wear it! But it's
dangerous, Sesame. In the wrong
hands, it can only do harm. You must
believe me!

Morbrecia's words echoed eerily in Sesame's head as the vision fragmented in a cascade of glistening charms. Sesame found herself back where she started – in front of the mirror, looking in. She felt a bit dizzy. She reached into her pocket for the photo of Poppy. Smiling back at her from the mirror was Zorgan and in his hand he grasped her locket!

Eight

Sesame stared at the mirror. Was the magician real, or was he just another illusion? Everything around her *seemed* real – the tower and the crescent moons above.

The peals of the gate bell sounded nine times and she knew time was slipping by fast. Zorgan sounded real enough too, when he spoke:

"Now do you understand, Sesame?" he said. He toyed for a moment with her locket. "You've seen what happened. If you want to help Karisma, you'll bring me the charms."

Sesame hesitated, thinking fast. I'm a Charmseeker! My quest is to return the magical bracelet to Queen Charm. At least, I thought it was. But maybe I've been tricked by the Silversmith? If the charms are cursed, perhaps I *should* give them to Zorgan? Oh, I wish I knew what to do! She looked at the magician patiently waiting, and knew she *had* to say something . . .

"Okay," she said slowly, pulling the photo of Poppy from her pocket. "But I want my locket. Now!"

Zorgan hissed. He held up his hand and the silver
locket glistened in the moonlight. His patience with
Sesame had run out and he could no longer disguise
his anger.

"Do you dare try to bargain with me?" he said, in
a chilling tone. "You may have your locket IF you
promise on your mother's name you'll bring me the
charms!"

Sesame shuddered at the venom in his voice. Holding tight to the photo she was aware of another, kinder voice echoing in her head: *Believe in yourself, Sesame. Believe in yourself.* And in that instant any thoughts she may have had about trusting Zorgan disappeared. She saw Zorgan for what he really was – a scheming, wicked magician!

"NO!" she yelled at him. **"NEVER!"**

What happened next took Zorgan completely by surprise. The locket in his hand turned scorching HOT. Without warning, the necklace shimmered with heat and burned his fingers – just as the magical charm bracelet had done, so many medes ago.

"OWWWOOOOOOO!"

howled Zorgan in agony. He flung the locket from the mirror and it landed at Sesame's feet. Before she knew what was happening, there was a blinding FLASH! She saw the crescent moons, reflected in the mirror shining so brilliantly they dazzled her. The beams were the brightest, fiercest light she had ever seen!

Stronger and stronger they blazed, until suddenly the mirror itself shattered into a million slivers of broken glass!

Sesame jumped back, shielding her face from the blast. When she looked up, she saw pale, ghostly shapes dancing for joy in the moonlight. From somewhere in the tower she heard Zorgan bellowing with rage, yelling for Nix and Dina. Moments later, she stooped to pick up her locket. It felt wonderfully cool to *her* touch.

"Brill!" she said, quickly slipping the photo of Poppy back into its place and putting the locket on. "I can't believe I've got it back." As she fastened the clasp with a *click!* she felt a familiar tingling sensation at her neck — the way her necklace always tingled when something extraordinary was about to happen. Her tummy flipped. She held her breath. Looking down she caught a tell-tale glint of silver, just where her locket had been when it had fallen. Bathed in gentle moonlight, where before it had lain hidden in the long, deep shadow of Zorgan's Tower, was the magical moon charm!

Sesame picked it up, allowing herself a moment to admire the perfect little crescent moon with its smiling face, before putting it safely in her pocket. Just then she heard the distant *clang* of the gate bell — ten strikes! Panicking, she knew she'd have to run like the wind to get back before the gate closed. Would she make it in time?

Clang! Clang! Clang! Clang! Clang! Clang! Clang! Clang! Clang! Clang!

Sesame was never quite sure what happened next, or how she found herself at the gate on the very last stroke of eleven. Everything happened so quickly.

She could still hear Zorgan yelling at Nix and Dina to go after her. Glancing over her shoulder, Sesame glimpsed their steely wings glinting in the moonlight, then she was running flat out, faster than she'd ever run before, her feet barely touching the ground. It was as if she was being carried along on a magical beam of light.

Meanwhile, behind her, brilliant moonbeams criss-crossed the path to block the pixies' view.

Even their sharp eyes couldn't penetrate the beams, and they soon lost sight of Sesame. Suddenly Sesame saw the gate . . . Quinch at the bell . . . clanging, clanging . . .

"Wait!" cried Sesame.

"Hurry!" shouted Quinch.

"Nine. Ten. ELEVEN!"

Sesame fell through the gate, tumbling down and around, over and over, through haze of golden stars until . . .

BUMP!

She tumbled out of her wardrobe mirror, back into her room.

Sesame sat on the floor, her head spinning, until Chips and Pins came out from under the bed and demanded her attention. She picked up the cats and gave them a cuddle, burying her face in their fur.

"Look," she said, showing them the mirror. "It's okay. The horrid magician has gone."

Leaving the cats to play, Sesame went to her jewellery box and opened it. The bracelet was there – ten charms securely in place. Carefully she took the silver moon charm from her pocket and fastened it with the others, so that now eleven charms glistened and shimmered radiantly with a magical light of their own.

"To think Zorgan nearly tricked me into giving them to him," she said. She smiled to herself. "No chance! I'm a Charmseeker. Sesame Brown will track the charms down . . . *and* give them back to the queen!"

She put the charm bracelet in the box and closed the lid, then unclasped her necklace and put it by her bed.

"Everything's okay now," she told her teddy, smiling.

Later, when Nic came up to say goodnight, he found Sesame tucked up in bed and half-asleep.

"Great film," he said. "Plenty of action. Sad ending. Jodie was in floods of tears! You okay?"

"I'm fine," she said sleepily. She yawned. She'd seen plenty of action herself this evening!

Nic caught sight of her locket on the bedside table.

"How did that get there? Did you find it in with your swimming things after all?" he said. "Where was it?"

But Sesame didn't answer. She had fallen sound asleep.

Nine

The Silversmith sighs as she looks at the thirteen magic candles. One more has flickered and gone out – it is the candle that bears the name of the crescent moon.

Now only two candles remain glowing, burning brightly until their missing charms are found.

She thinks of Sesame and feels once more a close bond with her Seeker, now that she has her locket back. She draws comfort from knowing that she played her part in thwarting Zorgan today. A little smile of satisfaction plays about her lips as she imagines how surprised he must have been to burn his fingers on the locket. And she is so proud of Sesame for seeing through his lies – he twisted the truth, but she wasn't taken in. She will see her quest through to the end, she is sure.

Only Zorgan stands in her path – Sesame has walked through his mirror of deception and defeated him this time . . . but she will have to face him again, and this time she may have to take him by force.

But that is another story. It must be told another day.

✾ ✾

✾

True or False?

Zorgan tried to confuse Sesame by twisting the truth, but she wasn't fooled by his tricks of deception.

Look in the mirror and see how much you know about the magical world of Karisma!

Which of these facts are true?

1. Princess Morbrecia stole the charm bracelet, because it was cursed and causing havoc.

2. The Silversmith mysteriously "communicates" with Sesame through her necklace.

3. Zorgan threw the charms away to destroy their Dark Energy.

4. Agapogo, the dragon, vowed to take revenge on the Silversmith.

5. Queen Charm is Morbrecia's younger sister.

Solution: 2 and 5 are true!

Acknowledgments

I owe a debt of gratitude to all those who have worked behind the scenes at Orion Children's Books and beyond to bring the *Charmseekers* books and their thirteen delightful charms to you. Since it would take more space than this edition allows to mention individuals by name, suffice it to say that I'm hugely grateful to my publishers and everyone involved with the publication of this series. In particular, my special thanks go to: my publisher, Fiona Kennedy, for her faith in believing I could write way beyond my own expectations. Her creative, tactful and skilful editing kept Sesame Brown on the right track and helped me to write a better story; my agent, Rosemary Sandberg; Jenny Glencross and Jane Hughes (Editorial); Alex Nicholas and Helen Speedy (Rights) Loulou Clark and Helen Ewing (Design); Clare Hennessy (Production); Jessica Killingley and Jo Dawson (Marketing); Pandora White (Orion Audio Books); Imogen Adams (Website designer – www.hammerinheels.com); Neil Pymer, the *real* Spinner Shindigs, for kind permission to use his name; and last, but by no means least, a million thanks go to my husband Tom for his inexhaustible patience, critical appraisal and support along the way.

Georgie Adams